WITZ & QUIZ

Karin Fritsch

More Fun with English Puzzles

Karin Fritsch

Karin Fritsch lebt in Weingarten und unterrichtet die Fächer Englisch und Deutsch an einem Gymnasium. Seit vielen Jahren setzt sie im Englischunterricht Kreuzworträtsel ein. Und da das ihren Schülern immer großen Spaß gemacht hat, entstand nach ihrem ersten Buch „Fun with Crossword Puzzles“ jetzt dieses zweite englische Rätselbuch.

In den Ravensburger Taschenbüchern außerdem erschienen:

RTB 3023
Fun with Crossword Puzzles

More Fun with English Puzzles

RAVENSBURGER BUCHVERLAG

Mit Bildern von Robert Erker

Originalausgabe
als Ravensburger Taschenbuch
Band 3065
erschienen 1999

Umschlagillustration: Robert Erker

RTB-Reihenkonzeption:
Jens Schmidt, Heinrich Paravicini

Printed in Germany

5 4 3 2 1 03 02 01 00 99

ISBN 3-473-53065-4

CONTENTS

WELCOME TO GREAT BRITAIN 7
HOW TO GET THERE 8
WHERE TO STAY 9
HAPPY LANDING 10
ENGLISH MONEY 12
FALSE FRIENDS 13
EVERYDAY DIALOGUES 14
FUNNY NAMES 16
LUCKY OR UNLUCKY ? 18
ANIMAL TALK 20
ABBREVIATIONS 22
ON THE ROAD 23
TRAFFIC LIGHTS 24
TRAFFIC SIGNS 25
A RHYME 26
SIGNS 27
TOUR OF BRITAIN 28
LONDON 30
AT THE SEASIDE 32
NESSIE 34
SCOTLAND 36
WALES 37
THE WELSH LANGUAGE 38
SHOPPING 40
JUMBLE SALE 42
SPORTS 44
THE WEATHER 45
WEATHER SYMBOLS 46
WEATHER FORECAST 47
THE SEASONS 48
SUMMER AND SUN 50

HOW TO MAKE A PHONE CALL 51
TELEPHONE PUZZLE 52
AT THE POST OFFICE 54
AN ENVELOPE 56
A POSTBOX 57
AT THE STATION 58
SETTING THE TABLE 60
AT THE TABLE 62
FOOD 63
ENGLISH BREAKFAST 64
BARBECUE 66
SANDWICHES 68
A THREE-COURSE MEAL 69
EATING OUT 70
A MAN AND A FORK 72
BIRTHDAY CARDS 74
BIRTHDAY TEA 76
BIRTHDAY PARTY (1) 78
BIRTHDAY QUIZ 80
BALLOONS 82
BIRTHDAY PARTY (2) 84
SAINT VALENTINE'S DAY 86
APRIL FOOL'S DAY 88
EASTER 90
EGG BASKET 92
CHRISTMAS CARDS 94
CHRISTMAS DAY 96
CHRISTMAS TREE 97
CHRISTMAS CRACKERS 98
SOLUTIONS 100

WELCOME TO GREAT BRITAIN

This is a map of Great Britain.

Write down the names of the countries in the boxes.

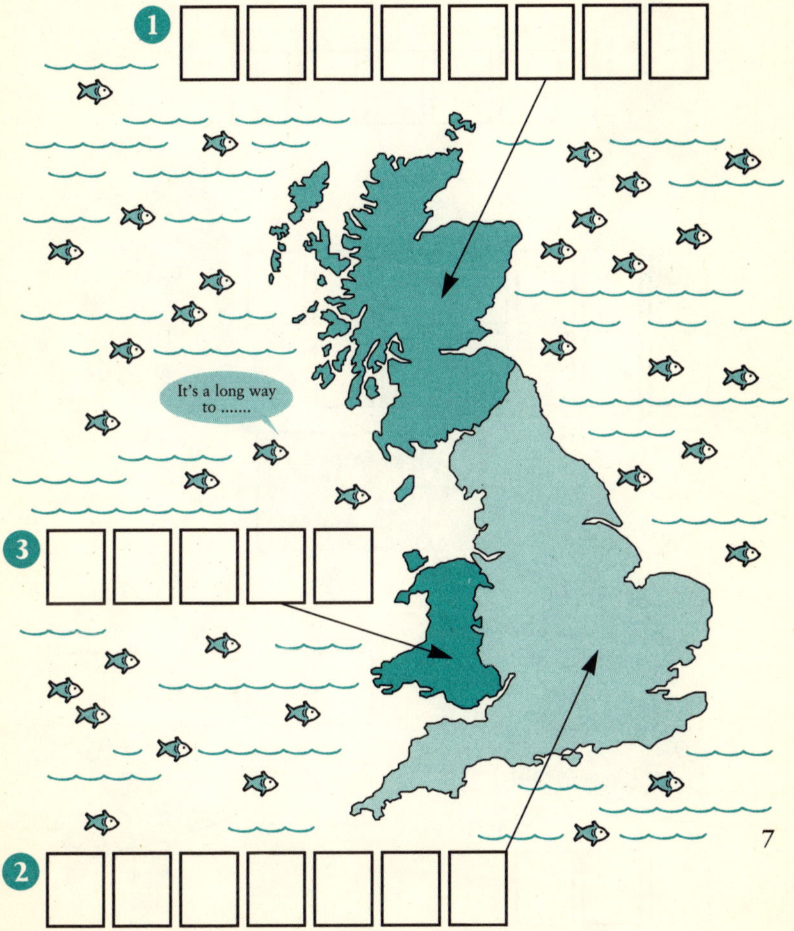

HOW TO GET THERE

There are different ways to get to Great Britain. Write down the names of the means of transport in the boxes.

WHERE TO STAY

These signs show you
where you can stay.
Write down the names of the places.

1.

2.

You can stay at a

4.

3.

HAPPY LANDING

The fastest way to go to London is by plane.
Find the correct word for each picture and write it in the crossword puzzle on the right. If your answers are correct you'll get the name of London's biggest airport.

AIRPORT

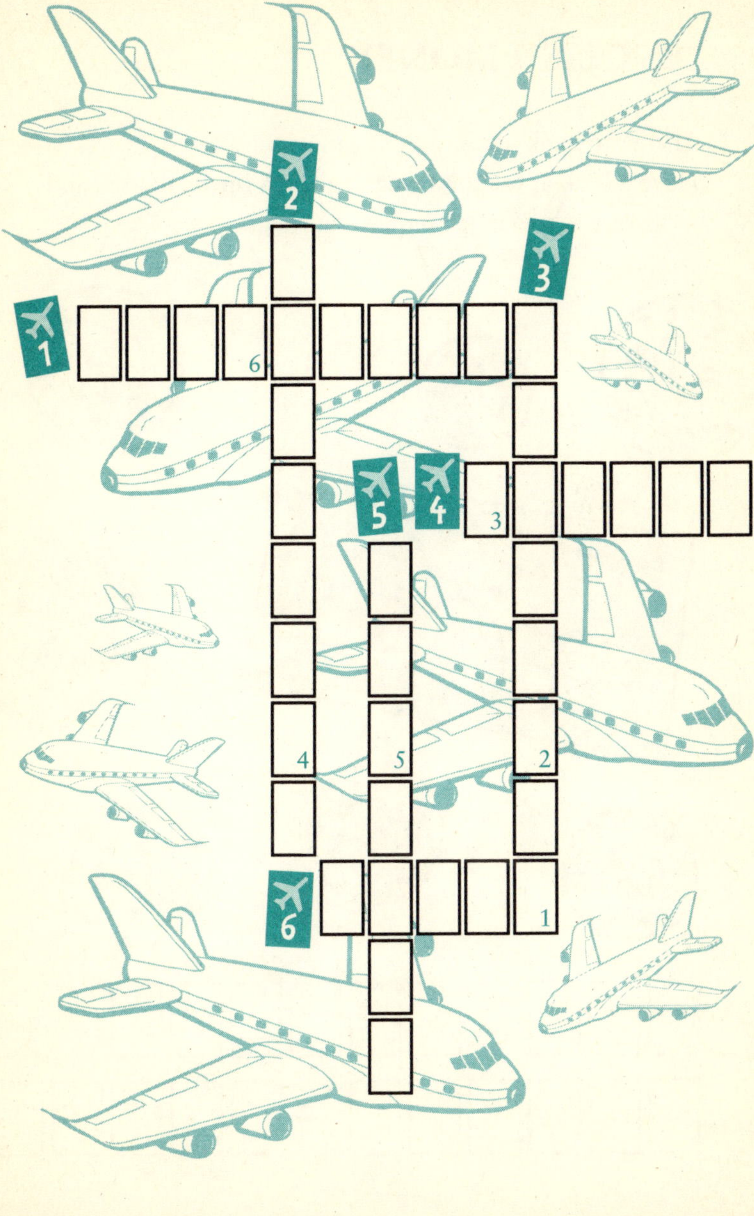
2
3
1
6
5
4
3
4
5
2
6
1

ENGLISH MONEY

There are bank notes  and coins. 
Have a look at the following coins and the bank note and write down how much money you've got.

FALSE FRIENDS

Do you know the meaning of these words?
Read the definitions and find the correct one.
Take the letter following the correct definition and write it in the numbered box. The letters will give you a new word – it's something that a winner gets.

1. A MAP

→ a plan P
→ a bag L

2. A Menue

→ a nice meal O
→ a list of food R

3. A chef

→ a cook I
→ a boss N

4. A gift

→ something that kills people G
→ a present Z

5. A bank

→ a place to sit down T
→ the place where your money is E

? = | 1 | 2 | 3 | 4 | 5 |

EVERYDAY DIALOGUES

What do you answer to the following sentences?
The sentences on the right will help you. Take the letter in front of the sentence and write it in the numbered box.

1. How are you?

2. Have a nice weekend.

3. Thank you for your help.

4. I'm doing a test at school tomorrow.

5. I haven't got a pen.

E Good luck.

A Thank you.
The same to you.

C Never mind.
You can have mine.

B You're welcome.

D Fine, thank you.

1	2	3	4	5

FUNNY NAMES

Do you know what these words mean?
Read the definitions and find the correct one.

1. Beefeater

= A person who only eats meat (A)

= A guard at the Tower of London (B)

2. Couch Potato

= A person who spends a lot of time in front of the TV (A)

= A meal made out of potatoes (B)

3. Bobby

= Nickname for a London policeman (A)

= a person who enjoys bob-sledding and other winter sports (B)

4. Union Jack

= Name of the British flag (A)

= Name of a big shop (B)

1	2	3	4

LUCKY OR UNLUCKY?

Did you know that some of these things are said to be lucky and others are unlucky? Look at the sentences and find the second part of each sentence on the next page.

A If you break a mirror ...

B If you are lucky at cards ...

D If you walk under a ladder ...

C If you find a four-leaf clover ...

A	B	C	D

1. ... you'll be unlucky in love.

2. ... you'll be unlucky.

3. ... you'll have bad luck for seven years.

4. ... you'll be lucky.

When is it
bad luck to have
a black cat
follow you?

When you're a mouse.

ANIMAL TALK

Do you know how English animal "speak"? Look at the pictures and find the correct sound for each animal. Write the letter in the box and you'll get the sound an English bird makes.

1	2	3	4	5

ABBREVIATIONS

An abbreviation is a short form of a word or words. For example, the letters "UK" stand for the words "United Kingdom".
Can you find out what the following letters stand for?

1

2

3

4

ON THE ROAD

In Britain cars drive on the left side of the road.
What must you do before you cross the road?
Write your answer in the boxes.

TRAFFIC LIGHTS

Before you cross the road you must wait at the traffic lights. Look at the sign, fill in the missing vowels (a, e, i, o, u) and you'll know what you have to do.

TRAFFIC SIGNS

There are a lot of traffic signs in Britain.
Do you know what these signs mean?
Fill in the missing letters
and you'll know.

1

N						
	Y	C				

2

R				D	A		O	U	T

3

T			

4

C			
P			

A RHYME

Can you find the missing words in this rhyme? Do you know who is speaking? Write your answers in the boxes.

I lie between
houses and □□□□□ ,
along me
busy traffic stops,
across me
people go their □□□ ,
I'm here
through every time of day.

? = □ □□□□

SIGNS

When you're in Britain you'll see a lot of signs.
Put the syllables in the right order and find the correct word for each sign.
Then take the letter following the word, write it in the numbered box and you'll know what people in London call the Underground.

1

WAY - MO - TOR (B)

3

PORT - AIR (E)

DER - GROUND - UN (U)

2

? = | T | 1 | 2 | 3 |

TOUR OF BRITAIN

Sam Smith is off on a tour of Britain, but which towns is he going to visit?

Take one box from the left and one box from the right to spell the names of six British towns.

Write their names in the puzzle on the right.

1	LON	DIFF
2	CAM	TOL
3	LIVER	GOW
4	BRIS	DON
5	CAR	POOL
6	GLAS	BRIDGE

1 LON
2 CAM
3 LIVER
4 BRIS
5 CAR
6 GLAS

LONDON

London is one of the most famous cities in the world and there are many things to see. Do you know the names of the following sights? Write them down in the boxes on the next page. When your answers are correct you'll get the name of the lake in Hyde Park.

1. The biggest church in London
2. It was a very famous prison
3. Name of the bell of the biggest clock in London
4. The biggest museum in London
5. Famous river that flows through London
6. The Queen's official home

1
4
2
3
3
2
6
4
8
10
5
7
1
6
9
5

AT THE SEASIDE

When you're on holiday in Britain, why not spend a day at the seaside? Write down the names of the things you can see in the picture on the right and you'll get the English word for the 7th thing.

Say this sentence as quickly as you can:

She sells sea-shells at the sea shore.

? = [₁] [₂] [₃] [O]

NESSIE

There is a famous monster living in a Scottish lake called Loch Ness: Nessie. Look at the questions on the right and write down your answers in the puzzle to find out what Nessie's favourite food is.

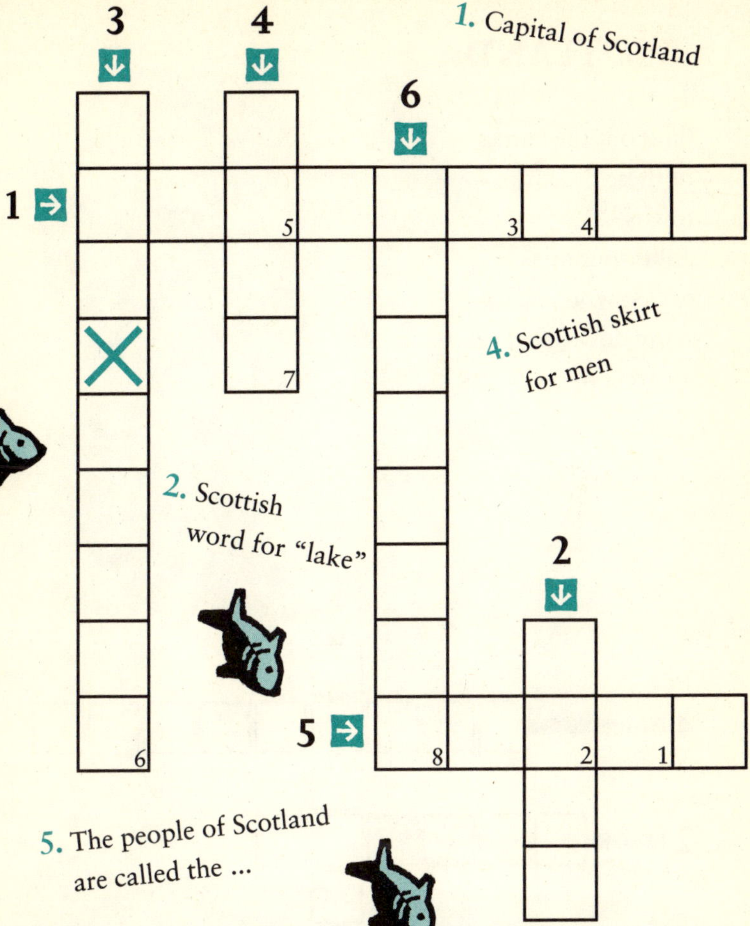

1. Capital of Scotland

2. Scottish word for "lake"

3. The highest mountain in Scotland

4. Scottish skirt for men

5. The people of Scotland are called the ...

6. Famous Scottish instruments

SCOTLAND

Find out the names of these Scottish towns.
Take your atlas to help you and write down your answers in the boxes.

WALES

The Welsh language is one of the oldest in the British Isles.
Road signs in Wales are given in Welsh and English.
This platform ticket shows the name of a Welsh village.
It has got a very long name.
How many letters has it got?

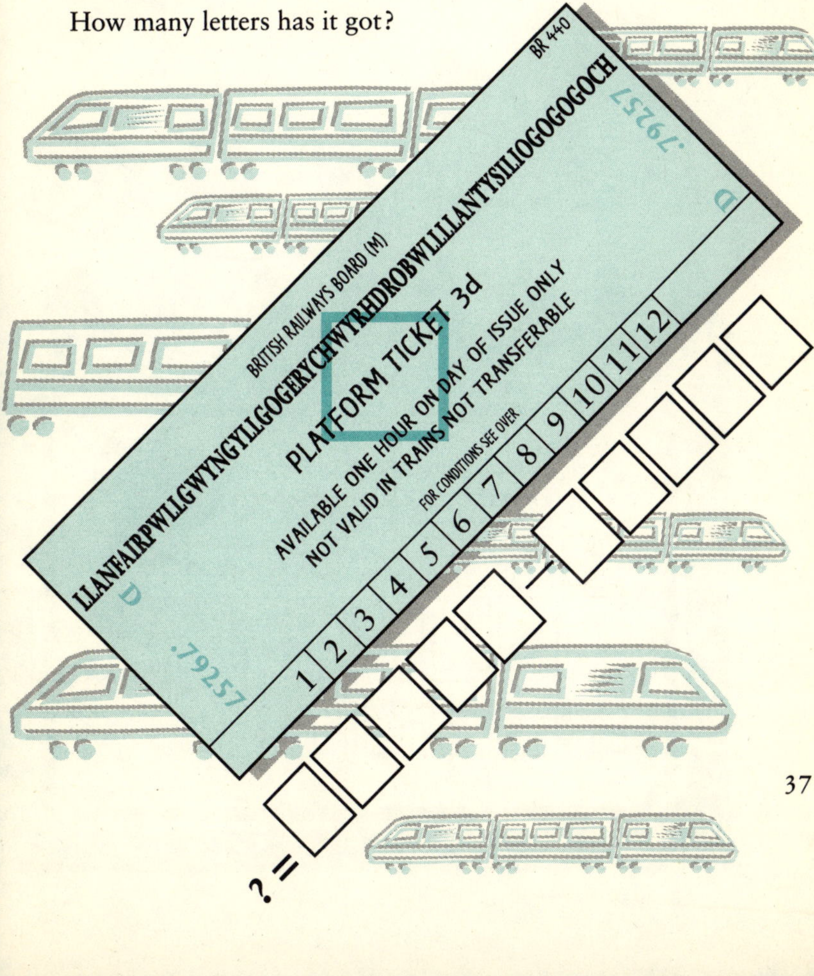

THE WELSH LANGUAGE

Do you want to learn Welsh? Answer the following questions about Wales and you'll know what "Welcome to Wales" is in Welsh.
Write your answers in the boxes on the right.

1 The highest mountain in Wales

2 There are many  in Wales

Welcome to Wales =

1	2	3	4	5	6	I
7	8	M	9	10		

3 Capital of Wales

5 Language spoken in Wales

4 A famous sport in Wales

SHOPPING

It's time to go shopping in an English town.
The supermarket is closed, so you have to go to different shops. Where do you get the things on your shopping list? Write your answers in the puzzle on the right.

Here is your shopping list:

You go to the

JUMBLE SALE

At a jumble sale you can buy old things. It's a good place for buying cheap things. How many things at this one begin with the letter 'B'? Find the words and the correct places where to write them down on the right.

1	B					
2	B			E		
3	B			K		
4	B			L		
5	B			O		
6	B			R		
7	B					
8	B					E
9	B					R
10	B					T

SPORTS

Many people in Britain like these sports. Do you know them? Write down your answers in the puzzle.
If your answers are correct you'll get the name of a game that can be played in most British pubs.

THE WEATHER

WEATHER SYMBOLS

What about tomorrow's weather?
Find the correct word for each symbol.

4

2

1

3

6

5

WEATHER FORECAST

This is a funny weather forecast. Put the letters in the correct order to find out more about Sunday's weather.

Most parts of England will be LOCD (2) and GOGFY (5). In the morning it will be RYD (1) but there will be a cold DIWN (3). There will be some NAIR (4) in the afternoon, so don't forget your RUMBELLA (6).

THE SEASONS

All these words have to do with the seasons. Find out if they belong to spring, summer, autumn or winter and find the correct places to write them.

camping
new leaves
ice-cream
thunder
A U T U M N
Easter
October
apples
W I N T E R
storm

SUMMER AND SUN

It's often very rainy in Britain. So British people really enjoy sunny days when they have them. Look at the pictures. Write the word for each picture in the boxes to make new words that all have to do with "sun".

4 S U N _ _ _ _ _ _ _

1 S U N _ _ _

3 S U N _ _ _

2 S U N _ _ _ _ _ _

HOW TO MAKE A PHONE CALL

Can you find the correct instruction for each picture? Then take the letter in front of the instruction and write it in the correct box.

TELEPHONE PUZZLE

In Britain there is a special number for calling the ambulance, the police or the fire-brigade. Find the missing words below and write them down on the right. If your answers are correct you'll get this special telephone number.

1
The ... is part of the telephone.

2
"Hello. Who is ...?"

5
The old English phone boxes were painted ...

4
"Listen. The phone is ..."

3
If you want to make a phone call, you need to know the ...

6
"Can you go and ... the telephone, please?"

TELEPHONE
? =
N
N

AT THE POST OFFICE

If you want to know what John and the clerk are talking about, have a look at the pictures.
Find the correct word for each picture and write it down in the puzzle on the right.

Good afternoon. I'd like five  (**A**) for 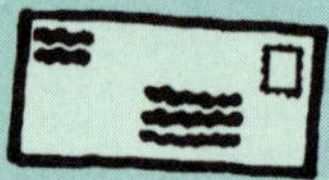 (**B**) to Germany, please.

Here you are. Anything else?

Yes, please. Can I have two  (**A**) for  (**C**) to Germany?

Yes, of course. It's the same for  (**B**) and 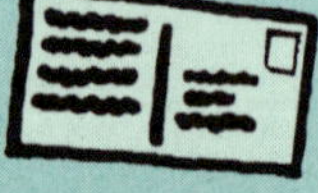 (**C**). But don't forget to write down the  (**D**) before you put them into the  (**E**).

C
D
A
B
E

AN ENVELOPE

Can you draw an open envelope without taking your pencil off the paper?

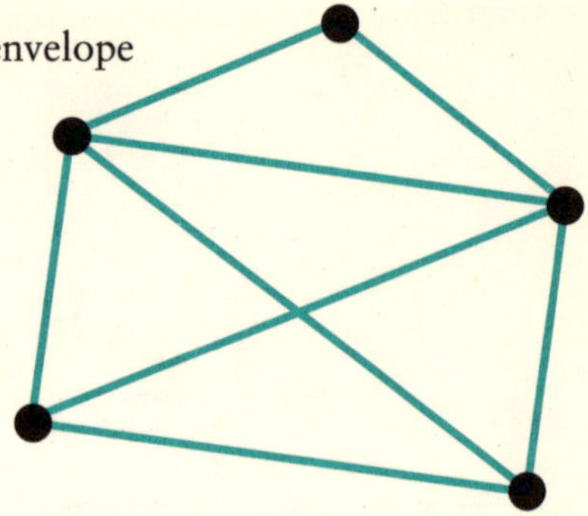

Start like this:

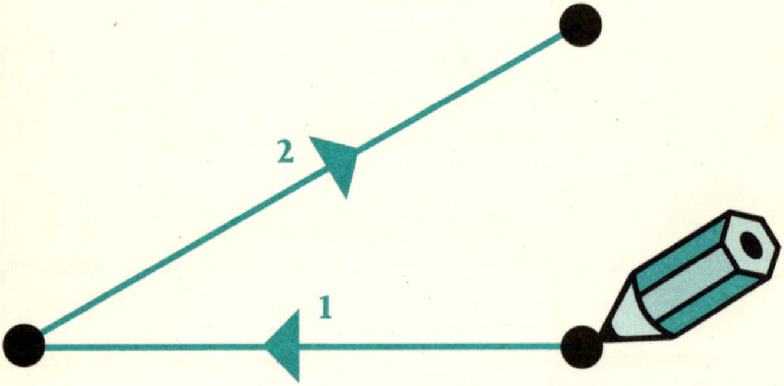

What travels around the world but stays in one place?

A stamp.

A POSTBOX

Look at the four words and find the correct places to write them. Then you'll know why Mr Black is angry.

1 POSTBOX

2 STAND

3 WHERE

4 MOUTH

Don't just (A) ☐☐☐☐☐

there with your (B) ☐☐☐☐☐

open. Tell me (C) ☐☐☐☐☐

I can find a (D) ☐☐☐☐☐☐☐

AT THE STATION

The missing words (???) all have to do with trains. Fill in the boxes on the right to get the name of London's biggest station.

1
You must wait for the train on the ???.

2
You look at the ??? to see when the train leaves.

3
The train from London usually ??? at 7.30 p.m.

4
You buy a ??? ticket when you want to go one way.

5
With a ??? ticket you can go to a place and come back again.

6
The next train to Glasgow ??? at 9.10 a.m.

7
Sometimes on a long journey you have to ??? trains.

8
If you want to go by train you need a ???.

? =

1	2	3	4	5	6	7	8

SETTING THE TABLE

The table has already been set for tea. Can you find the correct word for each picture? Write down your answers in the puzzle on the right and you'll get the English word for picture number "9".

1
8
7
3
5
6
2
4
9 =

AT THE TABLE

Can you find the correct answers to these questions?

1. Do you like the cake?
2. Can you pass me the sugar, please?
3. Can I have another biscuit, please?
4. Do you want a cup of tea?

1	2	3	4

A Of course, help yourself.
B Yes, it tastes good.
C Yes, please.
D Here you are.

FOOD

All these words have to do with food. Take one word from the left and one from the right to make new word pairs. Take the letter following the word and write it in the numbered box. The letters will give you a favourite English meal.

1. CHEESE
2. HOT
3. FAST
4. FISH
5. ROAST
6. FRUIT
7. CHIP
8. BAKED
9. BACON

DOG (R)
SALAD (F)
SANDWICH (B)
SHOP (A)
BEANS (S)
AND EGGS (T)
FOOD (E)
AND CHIPS (A)
POTATOES (K)

? =

1	2	3	4	5	6	7	8	9

ENGLISH BREAKFAST

In England you can have CONTINENTAL BREAKFAST or ENGLISH BREAKFAST. Continental breakfast means bread and jam with coffee or tea.
Look at the pictures on the right to find out what English breakfast is. Write down the names of the things in the boxes.

1 ☐☐☐

2 ☐☐☐☐

3 ☐☐☐☐☐

4 ☐☐☐☐☐

5 ☐☐☐☐☐☐☐☐

6 ☐☐☐☐☐☐☐☐

7 ☐☐☐☐☐☐☐☐☐

8 ☐☐☐☐☐☐☐☐☐☐

7
3
1
8
6
2
5
4

BARBECUE

In summer people often have barbecues. They barbecue pieces of meat, fish, vegetables etc. outside on a special grill that is heated by an open fire.
Find the correct word for each picture, write down your answers on the right and then you'll know what the Walkers are having to drink.

1							8	
2			1				2	
3							3	
4							7	
5				4	5			
6	6					9		

? =

W	1	2	3
4	N	5	
6	7	8	9

SANDWICHES

English people love sandwiches: cheese sandwiches, ham sandwiches, chicken sandwiches ...
Do you know who invented these famous sandwiches?

A ➜ Mrs Sandy Wiches
B ➜ The Earl of Sandwich
C ➜ A Baker from Sandwich

A THREE-COURSE MEAL

When you eat a three-course meal in a restaurant

you begin with a _ _ _ _ _ _ _ _ ,

then you have your _ _ _ _   _ _ _ _ _ _

and after that you choose your _ _ _ _ _ _ _ _ .

Find the correct places for these words.

MAIN COURSE

DESSERT

STARTER

EATING OUT

When you go into a restaurant in Britain, you usually wait at the door for the waiter or waitress to come up to you and tell you where to sit.
Have a look at the sentences on the right and write down your answers in the puzzle. Where there is a number in the puzzle, put the letter in the boxes below and you'll know what is written on the notice.

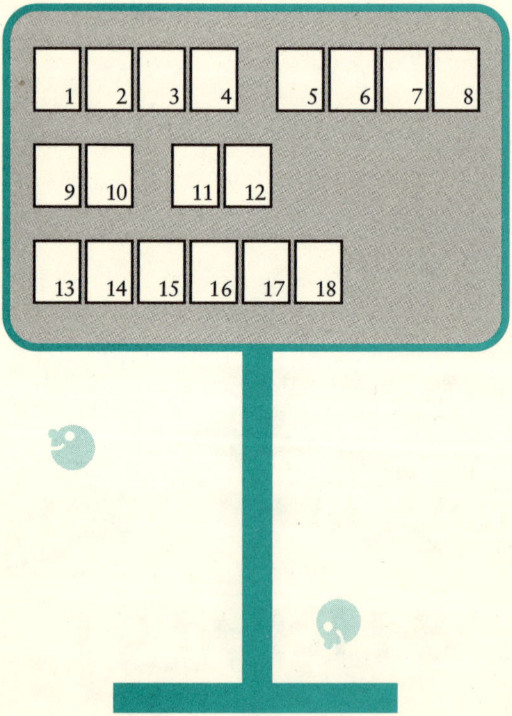

3. Where the meals are cooked

6. When you want to pay you ask for the ...

8. Cold drink

1. He works in a restaurant

5. Hungry and ...

4. Hot drink

2. Spoon, forks and ...

9. You eat it at the end of a meal

7. You eat it in the morning

A MAN AND A FORK

The following words are missing in the text on the right. Fill them in to learn more about the young man from New York.

ate

fork

was

trouble

apples ✔

man

cheese

New

There ______ a young ______

from ______ York

who ______ all his food with

a ______ .

He was o.k. with peas

and apples and ______ ,

but had terrible ______

with pork.

BIRTHDAY CARDS

Why not write a birthday card in English? Here are some ideas:

This birthday card is just to say - hope you have a wonderful day.

It's your birthday today.

Hip -
Hip -
Hooray.

It's your birthday.
Hope you have
a really
wonderful day.

Now it's your turn.

BIRTHDAY TEA

Jerry is having a birthday party with his friends. Put the letters in the correct order to find out what they are having to eat. Write down your answers in the boxes on the right and you'll know what they are having to drink.

1 _ _ _1 – _ _ _7 _ _
2 _ _ _4 _6 _ _ _ _ _ _
3 _ _ _ _ _ _
4 _ _ _ _ _
5 _ _5 _2 _ _ _ _ _ _ _
6 _ _3 _ _ _
? = L _1 _2 _3 _4 _5 _6 _7

BIRTHDAY PARTY (1)

Sue is having a party. Look at this picture for two minutes. Then turn to page 84 and answer the questions.

12
12
12
12
12

BIRTHDAY QUIZ

When is your birthday? Write it down here:

All these words have to do with your favourite day.
Can you find the right word for each picture?

4

3

5

2

5
3
6
2
4
1
6
1

BALLOONS

Look at the words in the balloons. It is difficult to read them because their vowels (a, e, i, o, u) are missing. Fill in the vowels and write down the words in the boxes to find out what Helen wishes her sister on her birthday.

4
FRNDS
2
HLTH
1
2
4
3
3
MNY

BIRTHDAY PARTY (2)

Can you answer these questions without looking at the picture again? Write your answers in the boxes.

1. How many girls are at the party?

2. It's Sue's birthday party. How old is she?

3. There are two animals at the party:

a ... and a ...

4. How many children are dancing?

5. What's Sue wearing?

a

6. What's Sue's father carrying?

SAINT VALENTINE'S DAY

February 14 th is an important day for people in love. They send cards or flowers to somebody they love. Often they don't write their names in the cards. So people must guess who sent them.
Here are three rhymes for Valentine cards. Some words are missing. Look at the words on the right and find the correct places to write them.

__1__ are red,
Violets are blue,
Sugar is __2__ –
And I love you.

To my Valentine

Lavender's blue, diddle-diddle,
Rosemary's __3__,
When I am __4__, diddle-diddle,
You shall be queen.

Wake up on this special __5__,
And __6__ these words from me.
It's not a dream. My love is true.
Look in my heart and see.

From your Valentine

1	2	3	4	5	6

APRIL FOOL'S DAY

On April 1st children and adults often play tricks on other people.
Even in newspapers you can read funny articles.
Have a look at the pictures on the right. Can you find the right word for each picture? If your answers are correct you'll know what you say to a person you've played a trick on.

7
2
4
5
6
3
9
1
8
1 >
2 >
3 >
4 >
5 >
6 >
7 >
8 >
9 >

EASTER

At Easter people give each other eggs, usually made of chocolate. Eggs mean new life and spring.
Fill in the crossword to find out the special name for Friday before Easter Sunday.

How many?

6

2

3

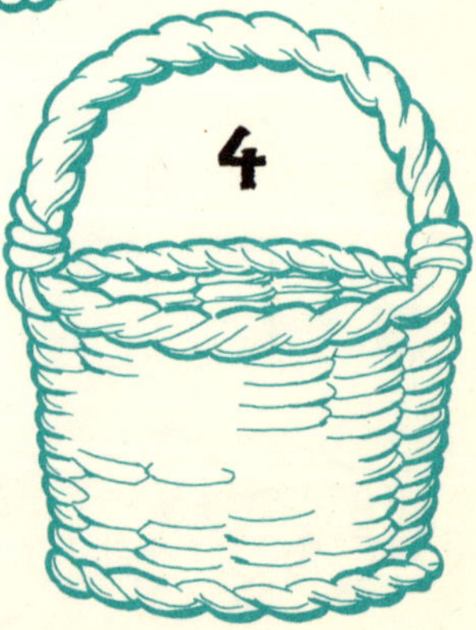

4

7 15th letter of the alphabet

5

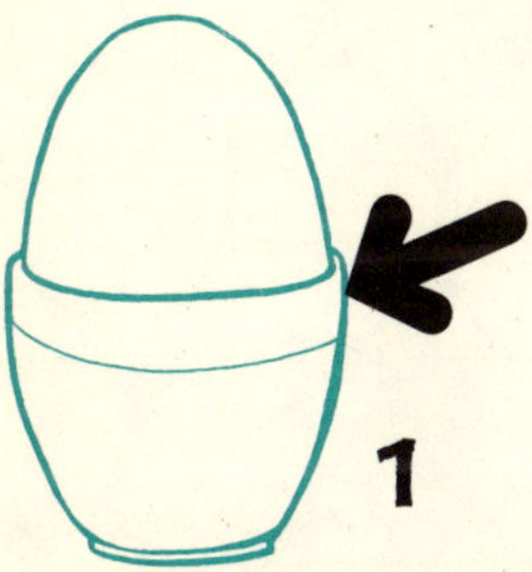

1

? = ☐ ☐ ☐ ☐ **Friday**

EGG BASKET

Write your answers in the basket.

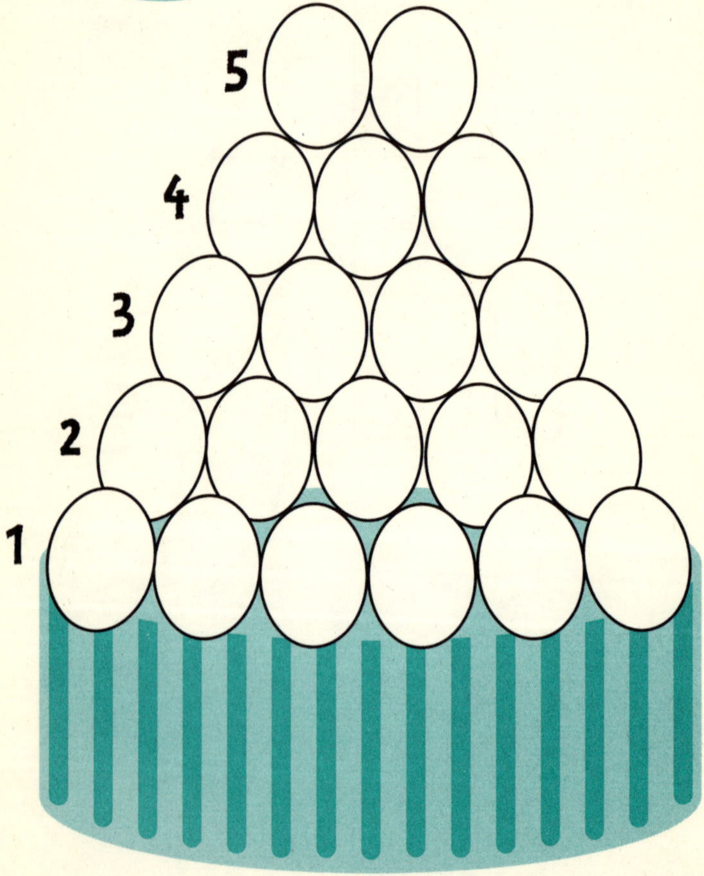

1

3

2

4

5 ... and down

CHRISTMAS CARDS

At Christmas people send cards to friends and relatives.
The cards say things like
"HAPPY CHRISTMAS AND A HAPPY NEW YEAR".
Look at the cards. Can you find out what they say?
All the vowels (a, e, i, o, u) are missing.
Write your answers in the boxes on the right.

1

3

2

To Carol and Jerry
HAPPY CHRISTMAS
from Ann xx
1
2
3

CHRISTMAS DAY

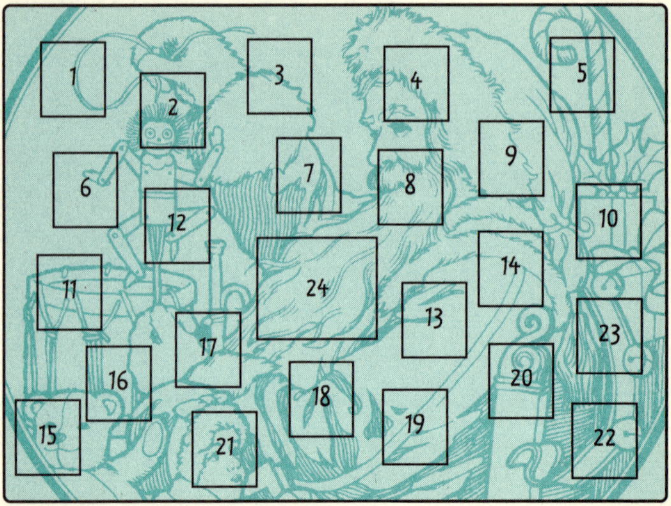

What are the following days called?

24 th December =

25 th December =

26 th December =

CHRISTMAS TREE

Some nice things are hanging in this Christmas tree. Find the right word for each picture and write it down in the Christmas tree.

CHRISTMAS CRACKERS

Before people eat their Christmas dinner they pull Christmas crackers. These make a loud noise and inside there is a small game or a toy and a ???

? = 1 2 3 4 5   6 7 8

Look at the following sentences and write your answers in the boxes on the right to find out what's in the Christmas cracker.

2. Another name for Father Christmas

7. British children hang up their  on Christmas Eve.

5. Father Christmas comes down the ...

6. British children get their presents on ...

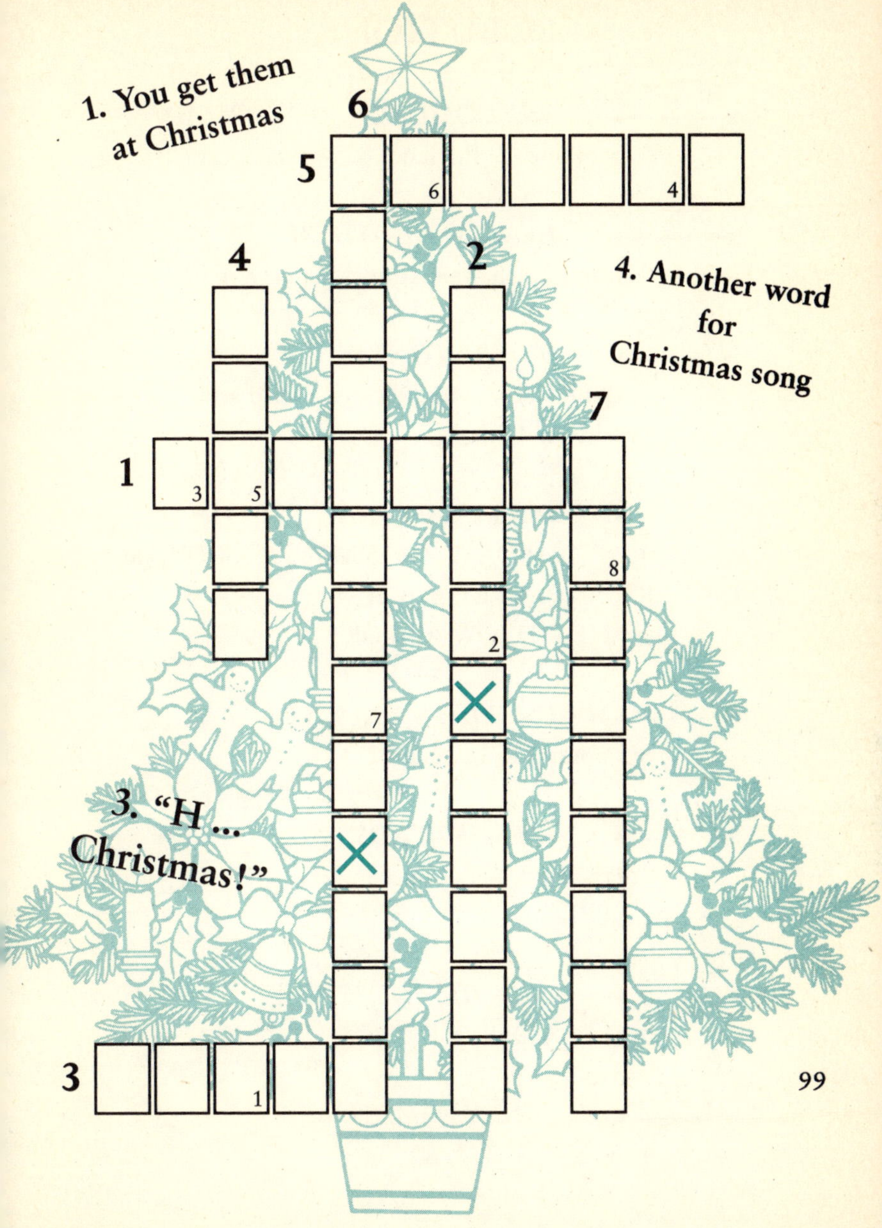
1. You get them at Christmas
6
5
4
2
4. Another word for Christmas song
7
1
3. "H ... Christmas!"
3

SOLUTIONS

p. 7

WELCOME TO GREAT BRITAIN

1. Scotland, 2. England, 3. Wales

p. 8

HOW TO GET THERE

1. train, 2. Channel Tunnel, 3. ferry, 4. plane

p. 9

WHERE TO STAY

1. camp-site, 2. youth hostel, 3. bed and breakfast, 4. hotel

p. 10/11

HAPPY LANDING

1. STEWARDESS, 2. PASSPORT, 3. SUITCASE, 4. TICKET, 5. TROLLEY, 6. PLANE

? = HEATHROW AIRPORT

p. 12

ENGLISH MONEY

Six pounds eighty-eight

p. 13

FALSE FRIENDS

1. P, 2. R, 3. I, 4. Z, 5. E

? = PRIZE

p. 14/15

EVERYDAY DIALOGUES

1. D, 2. A, 3. B, 4. E, 5. C

p. 16/17

FUNNY NAMES

1. B, 2. A, 3. A, 4. A

p. 18/19

LUCKY OR UNLUCKY?

A. 3, B. 1, C. 4, D. 2

p. 20/21

ANIMAL TALK

1. C, 2. H, 3. I, 4. R, 5. P

? = CHIRP

p. 22

ABBREVIATIONS

1. GB = Great Britain, 2. p.t.o. = please turn over, 3. L = Learner, 4. VIP = very important person

p. 23

ON THE ROAD

? = LOOK RIGHT

p. 24

TRAFFIC LIGHTS

PUSH BUTTON AND WAIT FOR SIGNAL OPPOSITE

p. 25

TRAFFIC SIGNS

1. NO CYCLING, 2. ROUNDABOUT, 3. TURN LEFT, 4. CAR PARK

p. 26

A RHYME

I lie between houses and SHOPS, along me busy traffic stops, across me people go their WAY, I'm here through every time of day. ? = a road

p. 27

SIGNS

1. UNDERGROUND (U), 2. MOTORWAY (B), 3. AIRPORT (E). ? = TUBE

p. 28/29

TOUR OF BRITAIN

1. LONDON, 2. CAMBRIDGE, 3. LIVERPOOL,
4. BRISTOL, 5. CARDIFF, 6. GLASGOW

p. 30/31

LONDON

1. ST PAUL'S CATHEDRAL, 2. THE TOWER,
3. BIG BEN, 4. THE BRITISH MUSEUM,
5. THAMES, 6. BUCKINGHAM PALACE
? = the SERPENTINE

p. 32/33

AT THE SEASIDE

1. BEACH, 2. DECK-CHAIR, 3. KITE, 4. SHELL,
5. SEAGULL, 6. CLIFF. ? = LILO

p. 34/35

NESSIE

1. EDINBURGH, 2. LOCH, 3. BEN NEVIS,
4. KILT, 5. SCOTS, 6. BAGPIPES.
? = TOURISTS are Nessie's favourite food.

p. 36

SCOTLAND

1. ABERDEEN, 2. DUNDEE, 3. GLASGOW,
4. EDINBURGH, 5. INVERNESS

p. 37

WALES

The name has got FIFTY-EIGHT (58) letters.

p. 38/39

THE WELSH LANGUAGE

1. SNOWDON, 2. CASTLES, 3. CARDIFF,
4. RUGBY, 5. WELSH. ? = CROESO I CYMRU

p. 40/41

SHOPPING

1. BAKER'S, 2. CHEMIST'S, 3. BUTCHER'S,
4. PET SHOP, 5. GREENGROCER'S,
6. BOOKSHOP

p. 42/43

JUMBLE SALE

1. BAG, 2. BIKE, 3. BOOK, 4. BALL, 5. BIRO,
6. BEAR, 7. BRUSH, 8. BOTTLE, 9. BLAZER,
10. BUCKET

p. 44

SPORTS

1. FOOTBALL, 2. HOCKEY, 3. RUGBY,
4. GOLF, 5. TENNIS. ? = DARTS

p. 46

WEATHER SYMBOLS

1. WINDY, 2. SUNNY, 3. RAINY,
4. CLOUDY / CLOUDS, 5. LIGHTNING,
6. THUNDERSTORM

p. 47

WEATHER FORECAST

1. DRY, 2. COLD, 3. WIND, 4. RAIN,
5. FOGGY, 6. UMBRELLA

p. 48/49

THE SEASONS

Spring: EASTER, TULIP, NEW LEAVES
Summer: ICE-CREAM, CAMPING, THUNDER
Autumn: APPLES, OCTOBER, STORM
Winter: CHRISTMAS, SNOWMAN, SKIING

p. 50

SUMMER AND SUN

1. SUNHAT, 2. SUNFLOWER, 3. SUNSET,
4. SUNGLASSES

p. 51

HOW TO MAKE A PHONE CALL

1. E, 2. A, 3. B, 4. D, 5. C

p. 52/53

TELEPHONE PUZZLE

1. RECEIVER, 2. SPEAKING, 3. NUMBER,
4. RINGING, 5. RED, 6. ANSWER.
? = NINE NINE NINE

p. 54/55

AT THE POST OFFICE

A. STAMPS, B. LETTERS, C. POSTCARDS,
D. ADDRESS, E. POSTBOX

p. 56

AN ENVELOPE

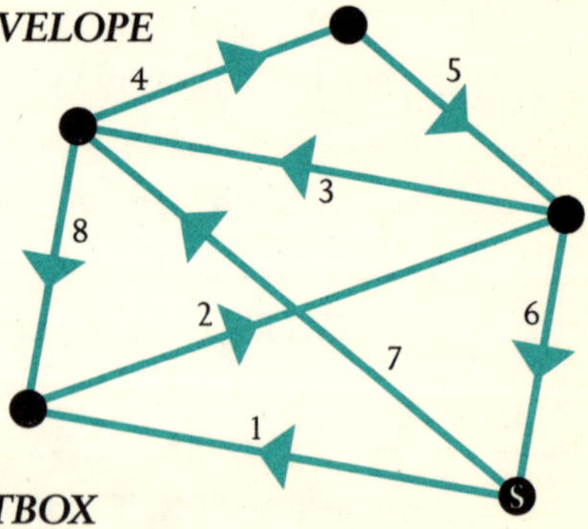

p. 57

A POSTBOX

A. 2, B. 4, C. 3, D. 4

p. 58/59

AT THE STATION

1. PLATFORM, 2. TIMETABLE, 3. ARRIVES,

4. SINGLE, 5. RETURN, 6. DEPARTS,
7. CHANGE, 8. TICKET. ? = VICTORIA

p. 60/61

SETTING THE TABLE

1. CUP, 2. SAUCER, 3. PLATE, 4. KNIFE,
5. FORK, 6. SPOON, 7. TEASPOON,
8. TABLECLOTH, 9. NAPKIN

p. 62

AT THE TABLE

1. B, 2. D, 3. A, 4. C

p. 63

FOOD

1. CHEESE SANDWICH (B), 2. HOT DOG (R),
3. FAST FOOD (E), 4. FISH AND CHIPS (A),
5. ROAST POTATOES (K), 6. FRUIT SALAD (F),
7. CHIP SHOP (A), 8. BAKED BEANS (S),
9. BACON AND EGGS (T). ? = BREAKFAST

p. 64/65

ENGLISH BREAKFAST

1. TEA, 2. EGGS, 3. TOAST, 4. BACON,
5. SAUSAGES, 6. TOMATOES,
7. MARMALADE, 8. CORNFLAKES

p. 66/67

BARBECUE

1. SAUSAGES, 2. CHICKEN, 3. POTATOES,
4. TOMATOES, 5. BREAD, 6. BUTTER.
? = WINE AND BEER

p. 68

SANDWICHES

B is correct. The Earl of Sandwich was a very important man in the American War of Independance. He liked playing cards very much but didn't want to stop playing in order to eat something. In 1762 he invented a snack: two slices of bread with something in the middle.

p. 69

A THREE-COURSE MEAL

When you eat a three-course meal in a restaurant you begin with a STARTER, then you have your MAIN COURSE and after that you choose your DESSERT.

p. 70/71

EATING OUT

1. WAITER, 2. KNIVES, 3. KITCHEN,
4. COFFEE, 5. THIRSTY, 6. BILL,
7. BREAKFAST, 8. LEMONADE, 9. DESSERT.
? = WAIT HERE TO BE SEATED

p. 72/73

A MAN AND A FORK

There was a young man from New York.
Who ate all his food with a fork.
He was o.k. with peas and apples and cheese,
but had terrrible trouble with pork.

p. 76/77

BIRTHDAY TEA

1. ICE-CREAM, 2. SANDWICHES, 3. CRISPS,
4. CHIPS, 5. HAMBURGERS, 6. TOAST.
? = LEMONADE

p. 80/81

BIRTHDAY QUIZ

1. PRESENT, 2. GUESTS, 3. CAKE, 4. HAPPY,
5. INVITATION, 6. CANDLE

p. 82/83

BALLOONS

1. HAPPINESS, 2. HEALTH, 3. MONEY,
4. FRIENDS

p. 84/85

BIRTHDAY PARTY

1. NINE, 2. TWELVE, 3. a CAT and a DOG,
4. FIVE, 5. a DRESS, 6. PLATES

p. 86/87

SAINT VALENTINE'S DAY

1. F, 2. C, 3. E, 4. D, 5. A, 6. B

p. 88/89

APRIL FOOL'S DAY

1. BISCUIT, 2. FLOWER, 3. BLOUSE, 4. STAMP,
5. WATCH, 6. FIRE, 7. DOLL, 8. BIRD,
9. PLANE. ? = APRIL FOOL

p. 90/91

EASTER

1. EGGCUP, 2. GARDEN, 3. SHELL, 4. BASKET,
5. HEN, 6. TWO, 7. O. ? = GOOD FRIDAY

p. 92/93

EGG BASKET

1. RABBIT, 2. SHEEP, 3. LAMB, 4. CAT, 5. UP

p. 94/95

CHRISTMAS CARDS

1. BEST WISHES FOR CHRISTMAS, 2. MERRY CHRISTMAS, 3. SEASON'S GREETINGS

p. 96

CHRISTMAS DAY

24th December = CHRISTMAS EVE,
25th December = CHRISTMAS DAY,
26th December = BOXING DAY

p. 97

CHRISTMAS TREE

1. STAR, 2. TINSEL, 3. BELL, 4. CANDLE, 5. ANGEL, 6. BALL

p. 98/99

CHRISTMAS CRACKERS

1. PRESENTS, 2. SANTA CLAUS, 3. HAPPY, 4. CAROL, 5. CHIMNEY, 6. CHRISTMAS DAY, 7. STOCKINGS. ? = PAPER HAT

Lies mich!

RTB Leseprobe

John Reynolds Gardiner

Stone Fox

A ten-year-old boy cannot run a farm. But you can't tell a ten-year-old boy that. Especially a boy like little Willy.

Grandfather grew potatoes, and that's exactly what little Willy was going to do.

The harvest was just weeks away, and little Willy was sure that if the crop was a good one, Grandfather would get well. Hadn't Grandfather been overly concerned about the crop this year? Hadn't he insisted that every square inch of land be planted? Hadn't he gotten up in the middle of the night to check the irrigation? "Gonna be our best ever, Willy," he had said. And he had said it over and over again.

Yes, after the harvest, everything would be all right. Little Willy was sure of it.

But Doc Smith wasn't.

"He's getting worse," she said three weeks later. "It's best to face these things, Willy. Your grandfather is going to die."

"He'll get better. You'll see. Wait till after the harvest."

Doc Smith shook her head. "I think you should consider letting Mrs Peacock in town take care of him, like she does those other sickly folks. He'll be in good hands until the end comes." Doc Smith stepped up into the wagon. "You can come live with me until we make plans." She looked at Searchlight. "I'm sure there's a farmer in these parts who needs a good work dog."

Searchlight growled, causing Doc Smith's horse, Rex, to pull the wagon forward a few feet.

"Believe me, Willy, it's better this way."

"No!" shouted little Willy. "We're a family, don't you see? We gotta stick together!"

Searchlight barked loudly, causing the horse to rear up on his hind legs and then take off running. Doc Smith jammed her foot on the brake, but it didn't do any good. The wagon disappeared down the road in a cloud of dust.

Little Willy and Searchlight looked at each other and then little Willy broke out laughing. Searchlight joined him by barking again.

Little Willy knelt down, took Searchlight by the ears, and looked directly into her eyes. She had the greenest eyes you've ever seen. "I won't ever give you away. Ever. I promise."

He put his arms around the dog's strong neck and held her tightly. "I love you, Searchlight."

And Searchlight understood, for she had heard those words many times before.

That evening little Willy made a discovery.

He was sitting at the foot of Grandfather's bed playing the harmonica. He wasn't as good as Grandfather by a long shot, and whenever he missed a note Searchlight would put her head back and howl.

Once, when little Willy was way off key, Searchlight actually grabbed the harmonica in her mouth and ran out of the room with it.

"Do you want me to play some more?" little Willy asked Grandfather, knowing very well that Grandfather would not answer. Grandfather had not talked – not one word – for over three weeks. But something happened that was almost like talking. Grandfather put his hand down on the bed with his palm facing upward. Little Willy looked at the hand for a long time and then asked, in a whisper, "Does that mean 'yes'?"

Grandfather closed his hand slowly, and then opened it again.

Little Willy rushed to the side of the bed. His eyes were wild with excitement. "What's the sign for 'no'?"

Grandfather turned his hand over and laid it flat on the bed. Palm down meant "no." Palm up meant "yes."

Before the night was over they had worked out other signals in their hand-and-finger code. One finger meant "I'm hungry." Two fingers meant

"water." But most of the time little Willy just asked questions that Grandfather could answer either "yes" or "no."
And Searchlight seemed to know what was going on, for she would lick Grandfather's hand every time he made a sign.

The next day little Willy began to prepare for the harvest. There was a lot of work to be done. The underground shed, where the potatoes would be stored until they could be sold, had to be cleaned. The potato sacks had to be inspected, and mended if need be. The plow had to be sharpened. But most important, because Grandfather's old mare had died last winter, a horse to pull the plow had to be located and rented.
It was going to be difficult to find a horse, because most farmers were not interested in overworking their animals – for any price.
Grandfather kept his money in a strongbox under the boards in the corner of his bedroom.

Little Willy got the box out and opened it. It was empty! Except for some letters that little Willy didn't bother to read.

There was no money to rent a horse.

No money for anything else, for that matter. Little Willy had had no idea they were broke. Everything they had needed since Grandfather took sick little Willy had gotten at Lester's General Store on credit against this year's crop.

No wonder Grandfather was so concerned. No wonder he had gotten sick.

Little Willy had to think of something. And quick.

It was now the middle of September. The potatoes they had planted in early June took from ninety to one hundred twenty days to mature, which meant they must be harvested soon. Besides, the longer he waited, the more danger there was that an early freeze would destroy the crop. And little Willy was sure that if the crop died, Grandfather would die, too.

A friend of Grandfather's offered to help, but little Willy said no. "Don't accept help unless you can pay for it," Grandfather had always said. "Especially from friends."

And then little Willy remembered something.

His college money! He had enough to rent a horse, pay for help, everything. He told Grandfather about his plan, but Grandfather signaled "no." Little Willy pleaded with him. But Grandfather just repeated "no, no, no!"

The situation appeared hopeless.

But little Willy was determined. He would dig up the potatoes by hand if he had to.

And then Searchlight solved the problem.

She walked over and stood in front of the plow. In her mouth was the harness she wore during the winter when she pulled the snow sled.

Little Willy shook his head. "Digging up a field is not the same as riding over snow," he told her. But Searchlight just stood there and would not move. "You don't have the strength, girl." Little Willy tried to talk her out of it. But Searchlight had made up her mind.

The potato plant grows about two feet high, but there are no potatoes on it. The potatoes are all underground. The plow digs up the plants and churns the potatoes to the surface, where they can be picked up and put into sacks.

It took little Willy and Searchlight over ten days to complete the harvest. But they made it! Either the dirt was softer than little Willy had thought, or Searchlight was stronger, because she actually seemed to enjoy herself. And the harvest was a big one – close to two hundred bushels per acre. And each bushel weighed around sixty pounds.

Little Willy inspected the potatoes, threw out the bad ones, and put the rest into sacks. He then put the sacks into the underground shed.

Mr Leeks, a tall man with a thin face, riding a horse that was also tall and had a thin face, came out to the farm and bought the potatoes. Last year Grandfather had sold the crop to Mr Leeks, so that's what little Willy did this year.

"We made it, Grandfather," little Willy said, as tears of happiness rolled down his cheeks. "See?" Little Willy held up two handfuls of money. "You can stop worrying. You can get better now."

Grandfather put his hand down on the bed. Palm down meant "no." It was not the crop he'd been worried about. It was something else. Little Willy had been wrong all along.

It's easy to tell when it's winter in Wyoming. There is snow on everything: the trees, the houses, the roads, the fields, and even the people, if they stay outside long enough.

It's not a dirty snow. It's a clean, soft snow that rests like a blanket over the entire state. The air is clear and crisp, and the rivers are all frozen. It's fun to be outdoors and see the snowflakes float down past the brim of your hat, and hear the squeak of the fresh powder under your boots.

Winter in Wyoming can be the most beautiful time of the year ... if you're ready for it.

Little Willy was ready.

He had chopped enough wood. They would not be cold. He had stocked enough food. They would not go hungry. He had asked Lester at the general store how much food Grandfather had bought last year. Then he had purchased the same amount. This would be more than enough, because Grandfather wasn't eating very much these days.

The coming of snow, as early as October, also meant the coming of school. But little Willy didn't mind. He liked school. However, his teacher, Miss Williams, had told Grandfather once, "Far as I'm concerned, that boy of yours just asks too many questions." Grandfather had just laughed and said, "How's he gonna learn if he don't ask?"

Then, later, Grandfather had said to little Willy, "If your teacher don't know – you ask me. If I don't know – you ask the library. If the library don't know – then you've really got yourself a good question!"

Grandfather had taught little Willy a lot. But now little Willy was on his own.

Each morning he would get up and make a fire. Then he would make oatmeal mush for breakfast. He ate it. Searchlight ate it. Grandfather ate it. He would feed Grandfather a spoonful at a time.

After breakfast little Willy would hitch up Searchlight to the sled. It was an old wooden sled that Grandfather had bought from the Indians. It was so light that little Willy could pick it up with one hand. But it was strong and sturdy.

Little Willy rode on the sled standing up and Searchlight would pull him five miles across the snow-covered countryside to the schoolhouse, which was located on the outskirts of town.

Searchlight loved the snow. She would wait patiently outside the schoolhouse all day long. And little Willy never missed a chance to run out between classes and play with his friend.

After school, they would go into the town of Jackson and run errands. They would pick up supplies at Lester's General Store, or go to the post office, or go to the bank.

Little Willy had fifty dollars in a savings account at the bank. Every month Grandfather had deposited the money little Willy had earned working on the farm. "Don't thank me," Grandfather would say. “You earned it. You’re a good little worker and I’m proud of you.”

Grandfather wanted little Willy to go to college and become educated. All little Willy wanted to do was grow potatoes, but he respected his grandfather enough to do whatever he said.

If there were no errands to run that day, Searchlight would just pull little Willy up and down Main Street. Little Willy loved to look at all the people, especially the “city slickers,” as Grand-father called them. Why, they didn’t know a potato from a peanut, Grandfather said, and their hands were as pink and soft as a baby’s.

You couldn’t miss the city slickers. They were the ones who looked as if they were going to a wedding.

At a little before six each day, little Willy would position his sled in front of the old church on Main Street. Today again he waited, eyes glued on the big church clock that loomed high overhead.

Searchlight waited too – ears perked up, eyes

alert, legs slightly bent, ready to spring forward.

B-O-N-G!

At the first stroke of six, Searchlight lunged forward with such force that little Willy was almost thrown from the sled. Straight down Main Street they went, the sled's runners barely touching the snow. They were one big blur as they turned right onto North Road. And they were almost out of town before the church clock became silent again.

"Go, Searchlight! Go!" Little Willy's voice sang out across the snowy twilight. And did Searchlight go! She had run this race a hundred times before, and she knew the whereabouts of every fallen tree and hidden gully. This enabled her to travel at tremendous speed even though it was getting dark and more dangerous.

Little Willy sucked in the cool night air and felt the sting of the wind against his face. It was a race all right. A race against time. A race against themselves. A race they always won.

The small building up ahead was Grandfather's farmhouse. When Searchlight saw it, she seemed to gather up every ounce of her remaining strength. She forged ahead with such speed that the sled seemed to lift up off the ground and fly. They were so exhausted when they arrived at the house that neither of them noticed the horse tied up outside.

Little Willy unhitched Searchlight, and then both of them tumbled over onto their backs in the snow and stared up at the moon. Searchlight had her head and one paw on little Willy's chest and was licking the underside of his chin. Little Willy had a hold of Searchlight's ear, and he was grinning.

The owner of the horse stood on the front porch and watched them, tapping his foot impatiently.

"Get over here!" The voice cut through the air like the twang of a ricocheting bullet.

Little Willy had never heard a voice like that before. Not on this farm. He couldn't move.

But Searchlight sure could.

The owner of the voice barely had time to step back into the house and close the door.

Searchlight barked and snarled and jumped at the closed door. Then the door opened a crack.

The man stood in the opening. He was holding a small derringer and pointing it at Searchlight. His hand was shaking.

"Don't shoot!" little Willy yelled as he reached out and touched Searchlight gently on the back. The barking stopped. "Who are you?"

"Name's Clifford Snyder. State of Wyoming," the man said with authority. He opened the door a little further. The man was dressed as if he was going to a wedding. A city slicker. He was short, with a small head and a thin, droopy mustache that reminded little Willy of the last time he'd drunk a glass of milk in a hurry.

"What do you want?" little Willy asked.

"Official business. Can't the old man inside talk?"

"Not regular talk. We have a code. I can show you."

As little Willy reached for the door, Clifford

Snyder again aimed his gun at Searchlight, who had begun to growl. "Leave that ... thing outside," he demanded.

"She'll be all right if you put your gun away."

"No!"

"Are you afraid of her?"

"I'm not ... afraid."

"Dogs can always tell when someone's afraid of them."

"Just get in this house this minute!" Clifford Snyder yelled, and his face turned red.

Little Willy left Searchlight outside. But Clifford Snyder wouldn't put his gun away until they were all the way into Grandfather's bedroom. And then he insisted that little Willy shut the door.

Grandfather's eyes were wide open and fixed on the ceiling. He looked much older and much more tired than he had this morning.

"You're no better than other folks," Clifford Snyder began as he lit up a long, thin cigar and blew smoke toward the ceiling. "And anyway, it's the law. Plain and simple."

Little Willy didn't say anything. He was busy combing Grandfather's hair, like he did every day when he got home. When he finished he held up the mirror so Grandfather could see.

"I'm warning you," Clifford Snyder continued. "If you don't pay ... we have our ways. And it's all legal. All fair and legal. You're no better than other folks."

"Do we owe you some money, Mr Snyder?" little Willy asked.

"Taxes, son. Taxes on this farm. Your grandfather there hasn't been paying them."

Little Willy was confused.

Taxes? Grandfather had always paid every bill. And always on time. And little Willy did the same. So what was this about taxes? Grandfather had never mentioned them before. There must be some mistake.

"Is it true?" little Willy asked Grandfather.

But Grandfather didn't answer. Apparently he had gotten worse during the day. He didn't move his hand, or even his fingers.

"Ask him about the letters," piped up Clifford.

"What letters?"

"Every year we send a letter – a tax bill – showing how much you owe."

"I've never seen one," insisted little Willy.

"Probably threw 'em out."

"Are you sure ..." began little Willy. And then he remembered the strongbox.

He removed the boards, then lifted the heavy box up onto the floor. He opened it and removed the papers. The papers he remembered seeing when he had looked for the money to rent the horse.

"Are these the letters?" he asked.

Clifford Snyder snatched the letters from little Willy's hand and examined them. "Yep, sure are," he said. "These go back over ten years." He held up one of the letters. "This here is the last one we sent."

Little Willy looked at the paper. There were so many figures and columns and numbers that he couldn't make any sense out of what he was looking at. "How much do we owe you, Mr Snyder?"

"Says right here. Clear as a bell." The short man

jabbed his short finger at the bottom of the page.
Little Willy's eyes popped open. "Five hundred dollars! We owe you five hundred dollars?"
Clifford Snyder nodded, rocking forward onto his toes, making himself taller. "And if you don't pay," he said, "I figure this farm here is just about worth –"
"You can't take our farm away!" little Willy screamed, and Searchlight began barking outside.
"Oh, yes, we can," Clifford Snyder said, smiling, exposing his yellow, tobacco-stained teeth.

Auszug aus dem Ravensburger Taschenbuch 2105 „Stone Fox“ von John Reynolds Gardiner.